The Perfect Cat-Sitter

The Perfect Cat-Sitter

by
Ann Whitehead Nagda

illustrated by
Stephanie Roth

HOLIDAY HOUSE / *New York*

Text copyright © 2007 by Ann Whitehead Nagda
Illustrations copyright © 2007 by Stephanie Roth
All Rights Reserved
Printed in the United States of America
www.holidayhouse.com
First Edition
1   3   5   7   9   10   8   6   4   2

Library of Congress Cataloging-in-Publication Data
Nagda, Ann Whitehead, 1945-
The perfect cat-sitter / by Ann Whitehead Nagda ;
illustrated by Stephanie Roth. — 1st ed.
p. cm.
Summary: When her friend Rana goes to India, Susan volunteers
to take care of her cat and her sister's fish, but the job turns
out to be much more difficult than she expected.
ISBN 978-0-8234-2112-1 (hardcover)
[1. Pet sitting—Fiction.   2. Cats—Fiction.
3. Schools—Fiction.]   I. Roth, Stephanie, ill. II. Title.
PZ7.N13355Pe 2007
[Fic]—dc22
2007018301

To Chas, Holly, and Dave
—A. W. N.

To the phenomenal
Mrs. Kris Guy
—S. R.

The Perfect Cat-Sitter

Chapter 1

Susan took out her notebook and opened it to a new page. She picked up the pink pen that matched her pink blouse and rosebud earrings. She was ready to take notes.

Mrs. Steele, her teacher, stood in front of the room. "Today we're going to start a new project," she said with a smile.

Susan smiled back. She couldn't wait to hear what Mrs. Steele had in mind. Her teacher thought of the best projects.

"As you may have heard, Rana and her family are going on a trip to India tomorrow." Mrs. Steele looked at Rana.

Rana sat in the seat right behind Susan. Susan turned around and stared at her. They had plans to go Christmas shopping over the weekend. Why hadn't Rana told her she wouldn't be able to go?

Rana was one of her best friends. Or at least Susan had thought she was.

Rana shook her head sadly. "I haven't told anyone yet," she said. "My grandfather had a heart attack yesterday. He's in the hospital."

Susan had met Rana's grandfather. He was such a nice man. She patted her friend's hand. "That's so scary, Rana."

"Is he going to die?" asked Kevin.

"I'm sure they'll take good care of him," said Mrs. Steele. "He's having surgery."

"We were supposed to go to Bombay over Christmas vacation, but now we have to leave right away," said Rana. "I'm worried about my cat, and my sister is worried about her fish. We have to find someone to take care of them."

Susan raised her eyebrows, looked back at Rana, and pointed to herself. She whispered, "I'll take care of your cat."

"Great!" Rana looked happy for the first time that morning.

"So we're all going to pretend to plan a trip to India," Mrs. Steele continued. "There are many different ways to get to India. You can go through Chicago or Los Angeles or New York. You can plan a stopover in Hawaii or Japan or Germany or some other country on your way. There are many different airlines that fly to Mumbai, which is the new name for Bombay."

"My grandparents don't use the new name," said Rana. "They still call it Bombay."

"Rana, how are you going to Bombay or whatever it's called?" asked Richard.

"I'll give Susan all the information about our trip," said Rana.

"That's great," said Mrs. Steele. "So, class, tomorrow we'll have Rana's itinerary."

"What's that? Some kind of suitcase?" asked Kevin.

"Does anyone know what an itinerary is?" asked Mrs. Steele.

Susan's hand shot up. "It's a plan for your journey," said Susan. "It lists your plane flights and the dates for each place you'll visit."

"That's right, Susan," said Mrs. Steele. "And I want each one of you to come up with an itinerary for your imaginary trip. You'll also make a map of your journey and figure out the total number of miles you'll travel."

"What if we travel more miles than anyone else in the class?" said Richard. "Do we get a prize?"

"That's an interesting idea," said Mrs. Steele. "We could have an award for the most miles traveled and the least miles traveled."

"What about an award for the most countries visited?" asked Richard.

"Good idea," said Mrs. Steele. "What are some of the places you'd like to visit?"

"I'd like to see tigers in India," said Mary.

"There are lions in India, too," said Rana.

"I thought lions were only in Africa," said Richard.

"India has the only lions left in Asia," said Susan.

"Then I'd definitely like to see those lions." Mary smiled at Susan.

Susan noticed that Mary was wearing a pink blouse, but her earrings were bright green. The pink and the green did *not* go together.

"I'd like to see the Great Wall in China," said Richard.

"Did you know you can see it from space?" said Susan.

"I bet she's been out in space," muttered Richard.

Susan sighed. Sometimes Richard was mean to her. She didn't understand why. She tried to be nice to him.

The bell for recess rang. Susan and Rana walked outside together.

"I'll let my mother know that you want to take care of my cat," said Rana.

"Tell her my mother will come sometimes to check on things," said Susan. "Just in case she's worried that I'm a little young."

"I'll tell her how responsible you are," said Rana.

"I will spend at least an hour a day at your house, keeping the cat company," said Susan. "Otherwise, Tiger could get very lonely."

"Could you feed the fish, too?"

"No problem," said Susan.

"I was so worried about leaving Tiger," said Rana. "You'll be the perfect cat-sitter."

"Of course," said Susan, smiling her biggest smile.

Chapter 2

When she got home from school, Susan set her pink backpack by the front door. Her cat, Portia, trotted down the hall and sniffed her pack. Her mother had named the kitty after a clever and determined character in one of Shakespeare's plays. "You're clever and determined, too, aren't you?" Susan cradled the cat in her arms and rubbed her chin on the cat's silky head.

Her mother called, "Hi, honey," from the dining room.

Susan called hello back and peeked in at her mother, who was reading intently. A pile of papers was stacked neatly beside her. Her mom taught two freshman writing classes at the local college and spent a lot of time grading papers.

When the phone rang in the kitchen, Susan put

the cat down and ran to answer it. "Hi, Rana. Yes, I'm sure. I really want to take care of your kitty. Let me ask my mom."

Susan held the phone against her chest while she walked back into the dining room. Her mother was writing all over a student's paper with red ink, but she looked up as Susan came in.

"Rana wants me to take care of her cat and her sister's fish while her family goes to India," Susan explained. "She wants us both to come over tonight. Is that okay?"

"How long will they be gone?" asked her mother. "The holiday season is such a busy time."

"Only two weeks, and they really need us," said Susan. "Rana's grandfather is sick."

"Okay, but it's a big responsibility," said her mother.

Susan made a face at her. If anyone was responsible, she was.

As soon as they finished dinner, Susan and her mother drove to Rana's house. Susan held a brand-new notebook. It had a red cover and was smaller than her school notebooks. She had labeled it "Cat-sitting at 801 Juniper."

"I'm so glad you're here," Rana said, and

motioned them inside. "My mother and father are going crazy, trying to get ready to leave tomorrow."

"I can imagine," Susan's mother said as she took off her coat.

"Throw your coats on the couch." Rana pointed to the leather sofa that already had a red jacket draped over the back.

"Oh," said Susan's mother. "I'll just hang them in the coat closet to get them out of the way." She put the coats on hangers and fastened several buttons on each.

Susan took a pen from her pocket and opened her notebook.

Rana led them to the kitchen pantry. "All the wet cat food is on the shelf. Tiger really likes tuna feast. But she'll eat the beef or turkey feast most of the time."

"How much should I give her?" asked Susan.

"Give her half a can a day. Sometimes she won't touch her cat food. She likes people food best. I often give her tiny pieces of chicken or hamburger or steak."

Susan made a note in her book. "Is it okay if I bring her a people food 'treat' now and then?"

"Tiger would love it! And she'll love you, too." Rana pointed to a blue-and-white bag with pictures

of cats on it. "The bag of dry food is on the floor. We let her eat as much of that as she likes. Fill up her bowl when it gets low. And keep her water bowl filled."

"Where is the kitty litter?" Susan asked.

"In the garage." Rana opened a door across from the laundry room and pointed to a big yellow bag.

Susan made some notes. "Where is her brush?"

"It's usually on the table by the television." Rana led the way to the family room. Newspapers and magazines were strewn across the table. She fished underneath the newspapers and found the brush.

Susan took it. "I'll put it next to the cat food, so I can find it."

Rana's mother entered the room. "Thank you both so much for taking care of the pets."

"My daughter will do all the work." Her mother beamed at Susan. "But I'll check on the house, too."

"Oh, and would you mind watering the plants once in a while?" Rana's mother walked over to the pots of ivy on the windowsill and stuck her finger into the soil. "Oh, my, these poor plants will need a drink soon."

"I'll take care of it." Susan turned to a new page and made a note about plant care.

Rana's little sister, Tara, raced into the room. "I'll tell you all about my fish. His name is Golden Boy." She took Susan's hand and led her upstairs. "I keep Golden Boy in my room. The door has to be shut so that the bad cat doesn't come in and eat Golden Boy."

"Don't worry," said Susan. "I'll keep the door closed."

Tara showed Susan the can of fish food. "You have to shake some of this in his bowl every day."

"Okay," said Susan, writing in her notebook. "I'll do that."

"What is the exact amount?" Susan's mother asked. "It's not good to overfeed a fish." She picked up the can and read the back. "Hmmm, it says one shake is enough."

"And you have to change his water every week," said Tara.

Tiger pranced into the room.

"No, Tiger," Tara shouted, "you can't come in my room."

Rana picked up the cat and held her close. "You don't like closed doors, do you? It makes you curious."

"Watch out for that sneaky cat," Tara told Susan.

"I will," said Susan.

"Write that down," said Tara.

Susan smiled and made a note in her book.

"We'll be home for Christmas, won't we?" Tara asked.

"No," said her mother. "We'll still be in India."

"We won't have a Christmas tree," said Rana, looking sad, "and the weather will be hot."

Susan felt sorry for her friend. She loved Christmas. It was her favorite time of the year.

"Oh, no!" Tara stood with her mouth open. "I'll

miss the holiday party at school. And I didn't get my fish a Christmas present."

"What kind of a present would your fish like?" Susan knelt down and put her arm around the little girl.

"Maybe some pretty rocks for his bowl." Tara looked very serious. "But they have to be clean."

Susan nodded and wrote in her notebook.

"I don't have a present for Tiger," said Rana sadly.

"How about a new catnip toy?" Susan's mother said.

"I'll bring some turkey from our Christmas dinner, too," said Susan. "My cat really likes that."

Tara looked up at her mother. "Did you pack my Christmas stocking?"

"Yes, dear," said her mother.

"Will Santa be able to find us in India?" asked Tara.

But both mothers were leaving the room, deep in conversation.

"Santa's pretty clever," Susan reassured the little girl.

When they went downstairs, Rana's mother showed them where all her house plants were. "My Christmas cactus is almost ready to bloom. Too bad we won't get to enjoy it."

"What about the bird feeder?" asked Rana.

"Maybe Susan could refill it once," said her mother. "The feeder is outside, next to the kitchen window. There's a trash can full of birdseed nearby."

Susan nodded. The job kept getting bigger and bigger. But she could handle it.

Rana's father sat at the kitchen table, studying his laptop computer. "The flight to Atlanta left right on time today. We shouldn't have any problems with our flights tomorrow."

"How long will it take to get to Mumbai?" Susan asked.

"About twenty-three hours," said Rana's father.

"Wow! That's a long time," said Susan.

"Bombay is nearly ten thousand miles away from here," said Rana's father.

Susan noticed that he didn't use the new name for the city.

"Dad, Mrs. Steele wants to see our itinerary," said Rana. "We're doing a travel project in class."

"I'll make a copy of it right now," said her father.

As Susan and her mother put on their coats to leave, Rana said, "E-mail me often. My dad's taking his laptop, so I can e-mail you from Bombay."

"I will," Susan promised. "Have a wonderful time and don't worry about a thing."

Chapter 3

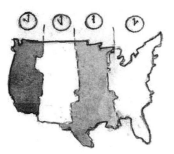

The next afternoon, Mrs. Steele stood in the front of the room passing out sheets of paper. "We're going to do some work today on airline timetables. This will help you with your imaginary trip. I'm giving each of you a copy of Rana's flights today from Denver to Bombay."

"Rana's father printed it out for me last night," Susan said. She felt very important.

"Too bad *you* didn't go to Bombay," Richard said in a low voice.

Susan turned around and stared at him. She wished he'd gone to Mumbai instead of Rana. And she was going to use the official name, Mumbai, no matter what anyone else called it.

"You'll notice that they will take three different flights," Mrs. Steele continued. "The first one goes from Denver to Atlanta. What time did that flight leave Denver?"

Richard raised his hand. "It left at eleven thirty A.M."

"That's right. It left this morning, didn't it?" said their teacher.

"Rana told me they had to be at the airport two hours early to check in all their luggage and go through security." Susan knew more about Rana's trip than anyone else in the class.

"What time does the plane arrive in Atlanta?" Mrs. Steele asked.

"It gets there at four thirty P.M.," said Susan.

"How many hours are there between the departure and the arrival time?" asked Mrs. Steele.

"Five hours," said Jenny.

"Yes. But look at what it says about the flight time." Mrs. Steele looked up. "It says the flight time is three hours. What happened to those extra two hours?"

"Maybe they had to sit on the runway a long time," said Kevin.

"That does happen," said Mrs. Steele. "But the time in Atlanta is different from the time in Denver—their time is two hours ahead of our time."

"When we drive to California, we always have to change our watches along the way," said Mary.

Susan noticed that Mary was wearing a blue blouse with earrings that matched perfectly. Of course, Susan had given her those earrings for her birthday.

"That's right," said Mrs. Steele. "The time in California is different from the time in Denver by one hour. Denver is in a different time zone from California or Atlanta."

Richard raised his hand. "Can I use the Internet to check on Rana's plane? I know how to do that."

"Go ahead," said Mrs. Steele.

Richard stood up, put his arms out like airplane wings, and zoomed over to the classroom computer.

Susan looked at Jenny and rolled her eyes. Richard was such a clown.

Everyone gathered around the computer. Susan was impressed. Richard really knew what to do. He went to an airline Web site and typed in the flight number. A map of the United States appeared on the screen.

"Rana's plane is over Alabama." Richard pointed to the screen. "This line shows the plane's route from Denver to Atlanta. And that small white

plane on the map shows you where the plane is now. It's almost over Georgia."

"The plane is flying at twenty-six thousand feet," said Jenny. "That's really high."

"That's about five miles above Earth," said Richard.

"Do you think her plane flew over our school?" asked Kevin.

"I don't think so," said Susan. "The school is west of the airport. The plane would have to fly east to get to Atlanta."

Kevin gave her a dirty look. Susan looked at him sternly. It was a good thing to know directions to places.

Mrs. Steele pulled down the map of the United States. "Class, please return to your seats now."

"Wait," said Richard. "The plane is losing altitude."

"What?" The teacher looked concerned.

Susan's heart started to pound. She rushed back to the computer. "Is something wrong?"

Richard continued speaking in his radio announcer's voice, as though he hadn't alarmed anyone. "The plane has started its initial descent into the Atlanta area. Everyone's tray tables should be stowed and their seats should be in the full upright position. The plane will be landing very soon."

"Very funny, Richard," Susan said, even though she didn't think it was funny at all.

"Okay, Richard," said Mrs. Steele, "we're all very relieved the plane is about to land. You can continue watching the flight for us, but I want everyone else to look up here." She picked up a pointer. "Here's Denver and here's Atlanta. Does anyone know the distance between the two cities?"

"About one thousand five hundred miles?" said Mary.

"That's a good estimate," said Mrs. Steele. "How could you figure it out more exactly?"

"You could use the Internet and ask Google that question," said Mary.

"That's one way," said Mrs. Steele. "Anyone else have an idea?"

"You could look at the scale on the map, measure the distance between the two cities with a ruler, and do the math," said Susan.

"Exactly," said Mrs. Steele.

"The airline website says it's exactly one thousand one hundred and ninety-six miles," Richard broke in.

Susan fumed. Now Richard was being Mr. Smarty Pants, but nobody made fun of him.

"That's another way," said Mrs. Steele. "When you plan your imaginary trip, I want you to mark each city you stop in on a map of the world. I also want you to make a brochure for one of the cities you visit, describing things to see in that city."

"What's a brochure?" mumbled Kevin.

"It's like a little booklet with writing and pictures in it," Susan told him.

"Okay, Miss Know–it–all," said Kevin.

Mrs. Steele stared at him. "Do we call people names?"

"Okay, Susan," said Kevin in a low voice.

Susan smiled. At least Mrs. Steele didn't let mean boys get away with things.

As soon as she got home from school, Susan logged onto her computer and started reading about Mumbai. She read about how the government changed the name of Bombay to Mumbai in 1995. Since Rana's itinerary called it Bombay, Susan decided she should mention both names in her pamphlet. Really, a visitor could get confused if someone said, "Welcome to Mumbai."

There were so many temples and museums and beaches in Mumbai. Her head was swimming with information. She needed to take a break.

Even though Rana's family had already fed the cat that morning, Susan decided to visit the kitty anyway. Cats were very sensitive creatures. She wondered if Tiger knew something unusual was going on when all her people left with suitcases.

After her mother dropped her off, Susan opened the big, shiny wooden door with the key and walked through the silent house. The refrigerator hummed in the kitchen. She checked Tiger's dish. The mound of wet food was all dried out and looked untouched. Outside the kitchen window, a chickadee visited the feeder.

Susan was surprised the cat hadn't come to the door like her cat always did. She looked in all the places downstairs where a cat might take a nap. Finally she went upstairs.

The cat was dozing on Rana's bed. Tiger opened one eye then shut it again. Susan stroked the kitty's fur, and Tiger opened both eyes and stretched. Then she hopped off the bed and smelled Susan's shoes.

Susan pulled her feet away. "Shoes are so dirty, kitty," she said. "You'll get dirt on your face." But the cat rubbed the side of her face on Susan's shoe. Tiger was a stubborn little thing. Susan sighed and gave in. The cat sniffed from the front to the back of one shoe then started at the front again.

"Can you tell where I've been, kitty?" said Susan.

The cat sat down on her shoe.

"Are you lonely?" Susan leaned over and patted the cat's head. "I brought you a treat." As she walked downstairs, the cat followed her. Susan opened a plastic bag that held a piece of meat loaf she'd brought from home. Tiger gulped down the meat loaf and looked up at her for more. "That's all I have today," said Susan. The cat sniffed her canned cat food, then backed away.

Susan followed the cat as it walked through the family room to the sliding glass door and looked out. There on the lawn was a small deer, standing perfectly still. Looped around the deer's antlers was a string of Christmas lights. The green wire holding the lights was twisted around both sides of its antlers and a loop of wire hung across the deer's face. Hanging behind one ear was another tangled loop of wires.

"Oh, you poor thing!" Susan said. She wondered what she could do to help but couldn't think of anything. She watched the deer for a few minutes, then decided to straighten up the coffee table. The house was a bit messy. She removed the newspapers from the pile and stacked the magazines in a neat pile on the table. There. The room looked better already.

She went back to the kitchen. Two cups and a dirty spoon had been left in the sink. She poured out the cold coffee and rinsed the cups. There was still a strong coffee odor. It was like the smell of her mother's freshly brewed morning coffee. She looked around the room. A red light glowed on the coffeemaker. Someone had left it on. Susan unplugged it. The glass carafe contained an inch of thick muddy coffee. She'd wash that out after it cooled. Rana's family was very lucky they had her taking care of their house.

The kitty coughed and ran to the family room. She crouched down and began to heave.

"Oh, no, kitty," said Susan, "not on the carpet."

The small cat heaved again and barfed up a mound of brown food.

Susan surveyed the yucky stuff. The cat had spit up all of her mother's meat loaf. "See if I bring you any more treats," she said as she hurried to the kitchen to fetch a paper towel. She grabbed a big spoon, too. Kneeling on the carpet, she scraped the vomit into the spoon, looking closely at it for hairs. Nope, there weren't any, so it wasn't a hair ball. Maybe bringing people food to the cat was not a good idea. Susan rubbed the stained carpet with the towel. She sighed. There was still a jagged brown circle on the tan carpet.

She looked under the sink for carpet cleaner. She moved a can of sink cleanser, a bottle of dish detergent, yellow and green sponges, and a box of dishwasher powder, and finally found a can of carpet cleaning foam. She read the directions carefully. She would need a damp sponge. She took a yellow sponge from the cabinet and wet it. Then she returned to the brown spot. Tiger watched her as she sprayed the carpet with foam. The cat stretched a paw toward the foam, but Susan hissed, "Don't you dare." The cat looked sadly at her and moved her paw back. Susan rubbed the carpet with the sponge. Rana and her family had only been gone a few hours, and already the cat had made a mess on the carpet. Susan wondered how many times the cat might throw up in the next two weeks. Fourteen times? She shuddered to think about it.

When Susan got home, she wrote an e-mail to Rana.

Subject: How was your flight?
From: Susan
 To: Rana
Tell me all about spending the night on a plane. Did you sleep much? How was the food? Did you watch a movie? I stopped by your house to visit Tiger today and she seemed very happy to see me.

Chapter 4

As soon as Susan entered the classroom the next day, she saw Richard sitting at the computer.

"Rana's flight from Atlanta to Paris was right on time," he announced. "And now she's on the plane to Bombay."

Susan walked over and looked at the computer screen. "It looks like they'll land in Mumbai on time, too."

Richard didn't answer. He had written three numbers on a sheet of paper. His pencil stopped at each number as he added them up. They were large numbers, so it took a while. Finally he spoke. "By the time Rana reaches Bombay, she will have flown nine thousand nine hundred and nineteen miles."

"Wow, that's impressive." Susan got out her

notebook and wrote the total down. "So it's one thousand one hundred and ninety-six miles from Denver to Atlanta, four thousand three hundred and forty-three miles from Atlanta to Paris, and four thousand three hundred and eighty miles from Paris to Mumbai?"

"That's right," said Richard. "It's four thousand three hundred and eighty miles from Paris to *Bombay.*"

Susan glared at him but wrote all the numbers down.

"Aren't you lucky that I'm doing some of your work for you?"

Susan gave him a big smile. "You're doing a good job, Richard. Be sure to check their flight later this morning. I want to know that Rana got to Mumbai safely."

"Aye, aye, Captain," said Richard. "Will do."

Susan wondered if he was making fun of her, but then he smiled.

Mrs. Steele took them to the library to do research for their brochures. Susan found a book about India, but it didn't give her information about places to see in Mumbai. She sat down at a computer, went to Google, and decided to do an advanced search for "sightseeing for children in Mumbai, India." She planned to e-mail all her brochure information to Rana and her family.

Richard was sitting at the next computer. He had found a website that gave him mileage between certain cities. He displayed the mileage from Los Angeles to Honolulu. It was 2,560 miles. He wrote that down on a wrinkled piece of paper.

"I thought we were supposed to be working on our brochures," said Susan.

"I am." Richard made a face. "I have to figure out where I'm going first."

Susan turned back to her screen. She read about the zoo in Mumbai, which had tigers, lions, bears, and monkeys. She made careful notes about that in her notebook. At the top of the page she had written "Mumbai Sightseeing." Next she read about boat trips along the coast. That sounded like fun. Riding a hot-air balloon over the city sounded even better. She wrote her notes on every other line, so that she could add more details later.

Richard erased something on his paper and swept bits of eraser onto Susan's lap. She brushed them away and watched him adding up six large numbers. He moved his hand down the page as he added.

"What are you trying to figure out?" Susan asked.

"The total miles to Bombay. I'm planning my trip through Los Angeles, Honolulu, Tokyo, Beijing, and Hong Kong on the way to Bombay."

"Why would you do that?" asked Susan.

"So I get more miles," said Richard. "And my trip will circle the globe."

"It would be easier to add all those miles if you write them neatly right under each other," Susan said.

Richard frowned, but wrote the numbers again.

"Now you could just add three numbers together, then the next three, then add the two sums," said Susan. "That would be easier, too."

"I'm going to do it my way," said Richard.

Susan shook her head. Richard was so stubborn. She looked around the lab. Several computers away, Kevin was typing on the keyboard while standing up. He was moving his lips to some soundless song in his head. She pushed back her chair so she could see his screen. There were several small planes displayed. It didn't look like he was working on his brochure either.

Mrs. Steele walked over to Kevin. "Do you need some help finding information?"

Kevin was easily distracted. He needed a lot of help. Susan turned back to her computer. She read about Juhu Beach, which had dancing monkeys, acrobats, and horse and donkey rides, as well as cricket matches. Susan pictured crickets on a tennis court. She would have to ask Rana about those crickets. Then there was a garden that only children and ladies could visit. That really sounded intriguing. And there were double-decker sightseeing buses. She had enough information to start her brochure.

"Wow! That's a lot of miles." Richard circled a number on his paper.

Susan read the number. "Eleven thousand five hundred and sixty miles." She noticed that Richard had used her method to add the numbers.

Later that morning Mrs. Steele said, "Rana should be arriving in India soon. Richard, will you check on the flight for us?"

"Sure." Richard sat down at the computer.

"So Rana's been in airports and in planes since yesterday morning?" Jenny asked.

"That's right," said the teacher. "It's a long way to India from here."

"Nine thousand nine hundred and nineteen miles, to be precise," Richard announced. "And you'll all be glad to know that the plane is on the tarmac in Bombay, where the local time is eleven thirty P.M."

"Don't you mean eleven thirty A.M.?" said Kevin.

"It's night in India now," Mrs. Steele explained. "India is about halfway around the globe from where we live." She picked up the globe and pointed to Denver and then to Bombay.

"But why is it night there when it's daytime here?" Kevin asked.

"Can anyone explain that?"

Susan waved her hand, but so did Richard.

Mrs. Steele nodded at Richard. "When Denver is facing the sun, the other half of the world is facing away from the sun," he said. "So it's dark in Bombay now."

Susan was miffed that her teacher had called on Richard instead, but she had to admit that he gave a good answer.

After school, Susan went to Rana's house. This time Tiger was there to meet her by the front door. As she walked to the kitchen, the kitten raced ahead of her. "You must be hungry, little kitty." Susan picked up a can of cat food. The cat sat looking up at her. She emptied the food onto a plate and set it down on the floor.

While the cat was eating, Susan went upstairs to feed the fish. Golden Boy was swimming around his bowl. When she sprinkled his fish food on the water, he came up and ate some of it.

She checked off two items in her notebook. On one page, she had listed the dates Rana would be away down the left side of the page. Then she had listed her chores across the top of the page: feed cat, feed fish, water plants, fill bird feeder. She checked the plants, but they didn't need water yet. The bird feeder was still full. Today she saw two house wrens pecking at sunflower seeds.

When she looked outside the family-room doors, she saw that the deer was back. He still had wires in his antlers.

Maybe if she approached the deer slowly with a pair of scissors, she could cut the wire that hung by his eyes. Susan searched the kitchen drawers until she found some scissors. She opened the sliding glass door and stepped out slowly. She didn't want to spook the deer. She closed the door behind her and stood on the patio studying him. He watched her, too. She took a deep breath and inched slowly toward him. He backed away. She walked closer. The deer stood frozen, looking at her with liquid brown eyes. She opened the scissors and went closer. The deer dashed around her and disappeared into the backyard. So much for that idea. She didn't realize that deer were such scaredy-cats. They always seemed so tame.

She turned to go back into the house. Tiger was sitting on the porch, sniffing the barbecue grill. Oh, no! The cat must have darted outside when she opened the door. "Come here, kitty," Susan said,

her voice trembling. "Please don't run away." But the cat dashed around the corner of the house. Susan raced around the corner, too, but Tiger was gone.

Chapter 5

Susan ran around the backyard, looking under all the bushes. "Here, Tiger," she called. "Here, kitty!" Her heart thumped in her chest. How could she have let the cat escape! That was so careless!

She hurried to the front yard. Juniper bushes lined the fence. She lifted a juniper branch so she could see behind it. Ouch! Now her hand itched. "Here, Tiger!" she called again. "Please come back, Tiger!"

Susan was getting really cold. She had to go inside and get her coat.

Maybe if she put out some food, she could lure the cat to the back porch. Her cat loved tuna. Probably all cats did. She'd open a can of real tuna, not cat food tuna. Her cat always raced to the kitchen when she smelled it.

Susan searched the pantry shelves for tuna. She moved cans over so she could see behind them. Behind tomato soup, she found a can of peaches. Things were all mixed up in Rana's pantry. Susan's mother always grouped things together. Soups were lined up, one behind the other. Cans of fruit were all nestled together, in an orderly fashion.

Hurray! She found a can of tuna. Now to find a can opener. Where could that be? Her hands were shaking as she searched through kitchen drawers. There it was! She grabbed it, put on her coat, stuck the tuna can in her pocket, and went outside. She set the can on the outdoor table, opened it, and looked around for the cat. Setting the metal lid on the ground, she dumped some tuna on it. Then, holding the can with the remaining tuna in it, she walked around the yard yelling, "Here, kitty! Tuna, kitty!" A squirrel scampered away as she walked by, but there was no sign of the cat.

Maybe Tiger was in a neighbor's yard. If Susan walked through the yards nearby, maybe the cat would smell the tuna and come to her. She looked into each yard first to make sure none of the neighbors were there. She didn't want anyone to find out that she'd lost Rana's cat. It was so embarrassing.

Susan walked through several yards, but the cat wasn't there.

Discouraged, she went inside to warm up. She didn't want to call anyone to help her look for the cat, because then they'd know how stupid she was.

She decided to search the Internet for information about finding lost cats. Rana's father had said she could use their computer. Susan read that indoor cats don't go very far. They are usually found within three houses of the owner's home. One website said to look on the roof, up in trees, and behind thick bushes. It also said to look under dark porches with a flashlight. Another one said to put smelly, dirty clothes outside. Sweaty socks were good. Susan remembered that Tiger was interested in her feet. Maybe socks were just the thing.

She went to Rana's room and found lots of dirty clothes. She sniffed the clothes and selected two pairs of socks, a sweatshirt, and a pair of jeans with something sticky on them. It looked like jelly. Susan didn't think the cat would be attracted to jelly. She carried the dirty clothes to the back porch. She could drip some tuna juice on the jeans. She shuddered. That would be icky and it might attract ants. But if it attracted Tiger, it would be worth it. She poured a little tuna juice onto the clothes.

This time, when Susan walked around the house, she looked up in trees and on the roof. No cat. She went through the neighboring yards, looking in the same places and calling for Tiger. Nothing. Without a flashlight she couldn't see under dark porches. How could she tell Rana that she'd lost her cat?

Susan sat down to think. She needed a flashlight, and she needed some help. If the cat didn't come back in five minutes, she'd call her mother.

She arranged the clothes into a nest on the back porch. She made a circle with the jeans. She folded the sweatshirt so that it formed a circular pillow inside the jeans circle. She tucked a sock on each side of the sweatshirt. She sniffed the nest she'd created. It smelled strongly of tuna.

She sat and waited. The cat didn't come back. Susan called home.

Her mother arrived with a flashlight, and together they walked through the neighborhood, shining the light under porch decks and behind bushes. Still no cat.

When they returned to Rana's house, Susan and

her mother sat on the couch together and stared out the window.

"Putting those dirty clothes outside is a good idea," said her mother. "So is the open can of tuna unless skunks or racoons come by and eat it. But it's probably too cold for them."

Susan sighed. "The cat has been gone a long time."

"I'm sure Tiger will come back." Susan's mother gave her daughter a hug.

"I feel so bad about this," said Susan. She could feel her eyes tear up.

"It was just a mistake," said her mother.

"I read that cats are sometimes lost for days," wailed Susan. "What if Tiger doesn't come back for days or weeks?"

"She knows that this is her home," said her mother. "Even if her people are away."

Susan's mother left to get some food for them to eat. Susan picked up a magazine and flipped through it, but she couldn't concentrate. She looked out the window. Something moved on the porch. It was Tiger. She was kneading Rana's sweatshirt with her paws. Susan smiled. Kittens did that on their mother's tummy. Sometimes, older cats kneaded their owner's lap or chest. Tiger walked in a circle around the sweatshirt nest, then sank down, curling into a furry ball.

Susan opened the door slowly. The cat looked up, but stayed where she was. Susan knelt down, talking softly. She held out her hand, and the cat sniffed it. Then she picked up the kitty and held her close. She carried her inside and planted a kiss on the cold fur of the cat's head. "I'm so glad you came home, Tiger."

Later, she brought the dirty clothes inside and locked the door. Carefully, she shaped the sweatshirt into a nest on the family-room carpet. It made the room look messy, but she thought the cat would like it. Sure enough, Tiger curled up on the sweatshirt and went to sleep.

Chapter 6

"I have a sample brochure to show you." Mrs. Steele held it out for everyone to see. "This brochure is about the Denver Zoo. On the front is the title, which is Denver Zoo, then underneath is a big picture of the entrance to the zoo."

"Do we have to have a big picture of our city?" Kevin asked.

"It would be nice," said Mrs. Steele. "See if you can find some pictures on the Internet."

"But what if we can't find any?" Kevin said.

"You could draw some pictures," said Mrs. Steele. She opened the brochure. "Inside this brochure there are pictures of the zoo as well as text."

"I might be able to draw animals," said Kevin, "but I don't think I can draw a city." He put his head down on his desk.

"This morning, I want all of you to do some writing for your brochures," said Mrs. Steele. "Make your city sound exciting, so that people who read your brochure will want to explore the museums and famous places. I want you to use lots of description."

Kevin moaned.

Susan looked over at Jenny and rolled her eyes. Kevin hated writing, which was hard to understand because writing was so easy. She took out her notebook and read her notes about Mumbai. Then she took a clean sheet of paper and started writing.

Mrs. Steele walked around the room and helped Kevin several times.

Richard clomped down the aisle to the pencil sharpener. He stopped by Susan's desk on the way back. He leaned over her paper. "Fascinating," he said, "just fascinating."

What a pest! Susan ignored him. She was still writing when Kevin threw his pencil down and leaned back in his chair.

"Let's read some of your writing out loud," said Mrs. Steele. "Why don't you start, Kevin?"

Kevin grabbed his paper and walked slowly

to the front of the room. "Bombay has lots of temples," he read. "You can visit them. It also has tons of museums. You can visit them, too."

"That's a good start, Kevin," said Mrs. Steele. "I want you to add some more details."

Kevin scowled.

"Can someone suggest some details Kevin could use?"

Jenny raised her hand. "He could tell the names of the museums and what's inside them."

"Good suggestions. Now who would like to read?" asked Mrs. Steele.

Susan raised her hand and walked to the front of the room. "Juhu Beach is the largest beach in India. Many film stars live there. On weekends, you can see acrobats and monkey shows. You can take pony rides or watch snake charmers and their snakes. The only thing you can't do is swim because the water is dirty."

"Very good, Susan," said Mrs. Steele. "Susan talked about specific things you can see on that beach, didn't she?"

Susan knew Mrs. Steele would like her writing. She always did.

"I already sent my description of Juhu Beach to Rana and her family," said Susan. "I hope they'll go there and let me know how it is."

Richard clomped to the front of the room next. "I'm writing about the Great Wall in China," he said. He cleared his throat. "The Great Wall of China is twenty-five feet high and it is made of stones and bricks. At one time it was more than three thousand miles long. It is also very wide. In some places it is thirty feet wide. Five horses could ride side by side on it. Can you imagine building something like that? The wall goes up and over mountains in northern China. You can walk along some of it, but there are a lot of stairs."

Mrs. Steele smiled. "You used lots of detail, Richard. I liked learning how high the wall is and also that five horses could ride side by side."

Susan was surprised. Richard's writing was almost as good as hers. Their teacher commented on two of his details. She hadn't mentioned any of Susan's. Maybe Richard's descriptions were even better than hers. She gave him a dark look as he walked back to his seat.

Mrs. Steele looked at the clock. "It's time for recess. We'll do more writing for your brochures tomorrow."

Jenny and Richard were standing together on the playground. Susan was walking past them looking for Mary when she heard Richard mention something about deer. "Do either of you have deer visiting your yard?" she asked.

"We had three last night," said Richard. "Three does were sitting in the moonlight. They looked like ghosts."

He even used good details when he talked. Susan tried not to be jealous. She needed information. "Have you ever seen a deer with Christmas lights wrapped around its antlers?"

"Sort of like Rudolph," said Jenny.

"But with glowing antlers instead of a glowing nose?" Richard wiggled his nose up and down.

"This isn't a joke," said Susan. "There was a deer in Rana's yard yesterday with a string of lights stuck in his antlers."

Richard gave her a puzzled look. "Now stand very still, Mister Deer, while I string some lights in your antlers." Richard shook his head. "Maybe a deer would stand still for Santa, but I don't know. . . ."

"The deer must have stuck his head in a bush or a tree that had lights strung on it," said Susan, "because the wire is tangled and hanging into his eyes."

"This I've got to see," said Richard.

"Me too," said Jenny.

"I'll call you when I see that deer again," Susan promised, "and you can come to Rana's house to see him, too."

"Great!" said Richard.

Afterward Susan worried about inviting people to her friend's house without permission. But they'd probably only stay for a few minutes. What harm could it do?

Chapter 7

When Susan arrived at Rana's house, she looked for the deer. Sure enough, the buck sat by some bushes, chewing his cud. Susan had read that deer eat quickly, then chew their food later when they're in a safe place.

She called Richard first. "The Christmas deer is in Rana's yard again."

"I'll be right over," said Richard, "and I'll stop for Jenny on the way."

The kitty rubbed against her leg. Susan put down the phone then knelt and rubbed the kitten's ears. "Poor hungry kitty. I'll feed you right now."

The small cat ran ahead of her to the pantry.

Susan had just scooped chicken feast onto a plate when the doorbell rang. She set the dish down and the cat bent over her food.

Susan hurried to the door as the bell rang again.

"Quick, take us to the Christmas buck," said Richard as he rushed inside.

Jenny followed him, rolling her eyes.

"Don't worry. The deer is still here," Susan told her friends. "You can see him through the window in the family room." She led them through the house.

The deer was still chewing.

"He must be a fairly young buck," said Richard. "He's got a small rack. I've seen one in my yard with much bigger antlers than that."

"The poor deer," said Jenny. "That wire hanging by his eyes must be very annoying."

"I went outside with scissors yesterday, but the deer wouldn't let me get very close."

"Hmmm," said Richard, "there must be something we could do." He looked out the side window, then went into the kitchen and looked out that window. "I think I have a plan. What's in that trash can by the bird feeder?"

"Birdseed," said Susan.

"There must be another can for trash somewhere."

"In the garage."

"If we move both of those trash cans in a line by the tree trunk, it would be like a fence. Then if we get the deer to come through the side yard, he'll have to go right under that tree limb." Richard pointed to the thick apple tree limb. "I'll climb up there with a knife or scissors and maybe I can cut that wire when the deer walks below the limb."

Susan nodded her head. "Scissors would be safer than a knife."

"How will you get the deer to walk through there?" asked Jenny.

"You and Susan will herd him," said Richard.

"Oh, boy," said Jenny.

"It just might work," said Susan.

"Jenny, you keep an eye on the deer while Susan

and I move the cans," said Richard. He went into the garage with Susan. "Ah, good, a ladder." He took the ladder outside and placed it against the tree trunk. He went back into the garage and tipped the trash can onto its two front wheels. The can rumbled as he moved it out the door. "What's the deer doing?" he whispered.

Jenny peeked around the corner of the house. She tiptoed back to Richard and Susan. "He looked up, but he didn't move."

Richard moved the trash can near the tree trunk. He carefully moved the can full of birdseed next to it.

Jenny peered around the corner again. "He's standing now," she said.

Richard climbed the ladder and inched his way along the tree limb until he was beyond the cans. He had his legs and one arm wrapped around the limb. He leaned down and took the scissors from Susan with his free hand. "I'm ready," he whispered, flicking the scissors open and shut. "Now get the deer to come this way."

"Be careful." Susan was starting to have second thoughts. What if Richard got caught in the deer's antlers?

But Jenny was already moving around the house to the back gate. She motioned for Susan to come along. The deer looked at them as they came through the gate. They waved their arms and the deer moved away. They moved closer, and the deer started to trot toward the side yard. As the deer approached the tree, Richard leaned down with the scissors open. He might even have touched one of the green wires on the antlers, but the deer jerked away, bolting up and over the fence just beyond the tree. With a cry of surprise, Richard fell on top of the nearest trash can, which toppled over. Richard lay still, his legs on the ground, his head and arms on the can.

Susan could hardly breathe. Her throat felt tight. She took a deep breath and knelt down beside him. "Are you okay?"

Richard gave her a crooked grin. "Umph," he groaned as he tried to get up.

Jenny grabbed his arm to help him.

Susan started to grab his other arm, but he cried, "Ow! Let go!"

He swayed as he stood up. "I don't feel so good," he said.

Susan had worried that this was a bad idea. She

should have known that the plan was dangerous. This was all her fault. Why had she let Richard get hurt? She took a deep breath.

"Lie on the ground." Susan took charge. "Take some deep breaths. Do you think your arm is broken?"

"It hurts a lot," he said.

"Don't move your arm." Susan stood up. "Jenny, you stay with Richard. I'm going inside to call my mother."

Susan told her mom about the accident. Her mother said, "Have Richard call his mother on your cell phone. Or you call her if he can't."

Susan gulped.

Her mother went on. "Don't move him. Grab a blanket and cover him, so he doesn't get cold. I'll be right there."

Susan found a blanket and hurried outside with it. After covering Richard, she held out her cell phone. "You should call your mother."

He grimaced.

"Do you want me to call?"

"Would you dial the number?" he asked.

Susan nodded. As Richard called out the numbers, Susan entered them on her cell. "It's ringing," she said.

Richard started to reach for the phone with his bad arm, groaned, then took it with his left hand instead. "Hi, Mom." Richard sounded almost cheerful. "Look, I fell out of a tree and I might have hurt myself." He stopped talking and rolled his eyes. "It's okay, really. No, nothing serious, but my arm hurts a bit. Well, I might be able to walk home."

"Give me the phone." Susan held out her hand.

"Mom, Susan wants to talk to you." He handed Susan the phone.

"Richard fell pretty hard, Mrs. Rogers. He cried out when I touched his arm. It might be broken. When he tried to get up, he felt dizzy." Susan paused and listened. "Yes, he's lying on the ground. I covered him with a blanket. My mom will be here any second. Yes, I think you should come, too. Wait. Here's my mother. Would you like to talk to her?"

Susan's mother rushed over. She knelt by Richard. "How are you feeling? You look pale. How far did you fall?"

"Not that far," Richard mumbled.

Susan pointed to the tree limb.

Her mother looked up. "Six feet perhaps? Maybe seven? That's a pretty good fall." She turned back to Richard. "Does anything hurt besides your arm?"

"My chest hurts a little," he said.

Susan held out the phone. "It's Richard's mother."

Her mother took the phone. "Yes, yes, I think we should call nine-one-one just to be safe." She nodded. "Yes, I'll make the nine-one-one call, and you just hurry over here. I'll tell them you're on the way. Yes, the address is eight-oh-one Juniper."

Soon an ambulance arrived, and a man carrying a box walked toward them. Behind him was another man as well as a police officer. The man with the box knelt by Richard and asked him, "What is your name?"

Susan started to answer for him, but her mother motioned for her to be quiet.

After Richard gave his name, the man asked, "What day is it?"

Susan made a face, but her mother whispered, "The man is an emergency medical technician, and he's making sure Richard is alert and knows where he is."

When the man asked, "What were you doing?" Susan held her breath.

But Richard answered simply, "Climbing the tree."

The man smiled, took Richard's pulse and blood pressure, and then put a plastic blow-up cast on his arm.

"Cool," said Richard as the cast inflated.

Later, after Richard's mother arrived, the man told her that he thought the only injury was a broken arm and perhaps some bruised ribs. But he wanted her to take Richard to the medical center to be checked out and have his arm put in a sturdier cast.

That night Susan sat down to write an e-mail to Rana. What could she say? Richard broke his arm falling out of your tree? Tiger got lost but then found again? No, that would just worry Rana's parents. They'd think she was a bad cat-sitter. Well, she was, wasn't she?

Subject: Tiger and Golden Boy
To: Rana
From: Susan

Tiger ate all her food today, then sat on my lap. Golden Boy ate a little food and swam around his bowl. Everything is fine.

Chapter 8

Susan woke up thinking about Richard and his broken arm. But she didn't want to talk to her mother about it. Her mother would probably say that it had been a bad idea to let Richard and Jenny come onto Rana's property.

Instead, she brought up another problem. "I'm still worried about the deer," she told her mother.

"Why don't you call the Division of Wildlife?" said her mother. "I'm sure they know all about our local deer and the trouble they get into."

"I'll call them this afternoon when I get home," Susan promised.

All during school, Susan worried about what she would say when she called. She wrote her questions on a new page in her notebook. Have other deer gotten things caught in their antlers? What happened to those deer? Should she set out some food for the poor deer in Rana's yard?

Before the class went to the computer lab to work on their brochures, Susan read her e-mail from Rana to the class. "Juhu Beach was great. We saw a movie company filming a scene. They had a big camera and microphones. The actresses wore beautiful flowered saris and heavy gold jewelry. Then my sister and I rode ponies, but we didn't get to ride very far. We saw a snake charmer with a big cobra in his basket."

"Did the snake bite anyone?" Kevin called out.

"I don't know," Susan said. "Rana didn't say anything else about the snake."

"Write back and ask her." Kevin made a snake head with his fist and pretended to strike Richard with it.

"Cut it out," Richard said, leaning away from Kevin. "My arm is already broken. I don't need a fake snakebite, too."

Susan cringed. She felt responsible for Richard's arm, which was now in a bright green cast.

Mrs. Steele shot Kevin a stern look.

Susan took a deep breath and continued reading. "My sister loved the monkey show best. One monkey wore a yellow jacket and pants and beat on a drum. The other monkey wore a dress and danced."

"Very nice, Susan," said Mrs. Steele. "You helped your friend have fun in Bombay. And it shows you how important a good brochure can be."

When the class went to the computer lab to work on their writing, Susan carried Richard's notebook for him. She stood next to him for a moment, but he said, "I'm okay. You don't have to stand there."

Susan sat down at another computer and brought up her file about Mumbai. She picked the

e-mail from Rana and read it again. It was the one thing that made her feel good. Using it, she added more details to what she had already written in her file—how one monkey danced while the other played a drum.

When Susan got home from school, her mother handed her the phone number for the wildlife department. Susan opened her notebook and dialed the number. "A deer in our neighborhood got a string of Christmas lights in his antlers," she explained. "Part of the wire is hanging near his eyes."

"Can the deer still eat and move around?" the man asked.

"I've seen him run out of the yard," said Susan. "And I've seen him eat some leaves."

"So the wire doesn't get in his way when he's eating?"

"No."

"That's good. We'd have to tranquilize the deer to remove anything from his antlers. That's more dangerous for the animal than just leaving the wires there."

"So you can't go near the deer while he's awake?" asked Susan.

"Deer can be very dangerous," said the man. "Don't ever go close to a deer. They may seem tame, but if they get scared, they can strike you with their front legs and injure you."

"Oh!" was all Susan could say. She'd had no idea deer could hurt you. Richard was lucky he'd only broken his arm. It could have been worse.

"Male deer often get things caught in their antlers," the man continued. "One deer even had a yellow rope and a child's swing hanging from one antler. We usually allow nature to take its course unless the deer is suffering a lot. The deer's antlers should fall off naturally in the next month or two."

Susan took notes on what the man told her. She glanced at her list. She had one more question. "What about setting out some food for the deer?"

"That's a very bad idea. Feeding any big-game animal like deer is illegal in Colorado and in many other states."

The man sounded a bit angry. Susan felt like a criminal. She'd tossed an apple outside for the deer. It was a good thing she hadn't mentioned that.

The man continued to explain in a more kindly voice. "You see, deer are naturally wild, but if they become accustomed to humans, they lose their nat-

ural fear. Besides, many things that people offer deer, like bread or hay, aren't good for them."

Well, at least Susan had given the deer a healthy snack. After she said thank you and good-bye to the man, she dropped into a chair, shut her eyes, and sat with her face cradled in both hands. She thought she was so smart, but she was really an utter failure.

Chapter 9

The next day Susan put the finishing touches on her brochure. She had finished all her writing about Mumbai and had put several pictures in her document already. She just needed one more. After inserting a picture of Juhu Beach, she sent the file to the printer. The school had a black-and-white printer. It was good enough for the first draft, but she was going to print her final version on her home printer. It printed in color.

As Susan walked back to her computer, she looked at the screens of other students. Kevin had pictures of race cars on his computer. "I didn't know they raced cars in India," Susan said.

Kevin shot her a dirty look.

Susan sat down in front of her computer and saved her file on her flash drive. She turned and watched Richard, who sat beside her. He was typing with one finger. He wasn't using the hand from his broken arm. Susan had a funny feeling in her stomach every time she looked at his bright green cast. "Does your arm hurt?" she asked him.

"A little." Richard held his arm close to his body.

"I can help you with your brochure." Susan moved her chair closer to Richard's. "I can put some pictures in your document."

"That would be great." Richard stood up and switched chairs with Susan.

"If you made your margins smaller, you could make a four-page brochure like mine," Susan said. "I'm going to take a sheet of colored construction paper and fold it in half. Then I'm going to cut up my computer printout and glue it onto the construction paper."

"I don't know if I can do that," said Richard. "I'm pretty clumsy with my arm in this cast."

Susan cringed. "I'll help you," she said. "You can come to my house after school. Jenny can come, too."

Jenny looked up. She was sitting on Richard's other side. "Sure, we'll both help you."

"I don't know," said Richard.

"I want to help you." Susan looked down at Richard's arm. "It's my fault you broke your arm."

"Not really," Richard began.

"Yes, really," said Susan. "And I want to make it up to you."

Richard shrugged. "Okay," he said.

When Susan got home from school, she logged onto the Internet. Portia sat on her lap while she checked her e-mail. Susan read a new message from Rana. "It doesn't feel like Christmas here. I miss the cold weather and snow and Christmas lights on people's houses. I miss the piney smell of a Christmas tree and the fun of hanging ornaments on it. I miss Christmas carols playing while we wrap presents. And my sister, Tara, is afraid that Santa will never find us here. She's afraid her stocking will be empty on Christmas morning."

Susan felt sorry for her friend, but she didn't know what to write back. She could say, "I'm glad I can enjoy all those things," but that wouldn't be nice. She could write, "Christmas lights are nice, unless they get stuck in a deer's antlers," but that would require a lot of explanation. Maybe she'd wait until later to send a reply.

Instead, she worked on getting ready for Richard and Jenny. First she printed out her brochure pages on the color printer. They looked great. Susan felt a warm glow inside her chest. She loved doing a good job. She loaded Richard's brochure information from her flash drive and looked it over. She found several spelling errors and corrected them. The Great Wall picture that she and Richard had selected in the computer lab wasn't that good. She searched the Internet and found a better one. But perhaps she should ask him if he liked the new picture before she put it in his brochure. She wanted to help Richard make a really good brochure. Maybe then she wouldn't feel so guilty about his broken arm.

Susan held Portia while she stood up, then set her on the chair seat. The cat jumped down and pranced out of the room. Fussy cat. Susan got out construction paper, rubber cement, scissors, and a ruler. She carried them all to the kitchen table. She spread several pages of newspaper on one area of the table. That's where they'd use the rubber cement. She put a paper towel next to the newspaper for wiping glue from sticky fingers.

She ran upstairs to use the paper cutter and cut off the excess paper around each part of her brochure. While she waited for Richard and Jenny to arrive, she would start to put her brochure together. Susan looked through the different colors of construction paper, holding a light blue sheet next to her pictures. No, for India she needed a vibrant color like red or orange or yellow. She finally decided on the red paper. She drew a faint line in pencil on the construction paper, so that she could leave a one-inch margin at the bottom of the page. Then she put rubber cement on the front section of her printout and pressed it onto the red construction paper. By the time Jenny arrived, Susan had finished her brochure.

"Wow! That looks great!" said Jenny.

Susan smiled. "What color would you like to use?"

"Yellow," said Jenny.

When Richard arrived, Susan showed him the new picture she had found. "Do you like this one?"

"I think you should use that picture," Jenny said.

Richard agreed, so Susan inserted the new picture and then printed out his pages.

"I brought my file with me," said Jenny.

Susan printed the pages for Jenny's brochure while Jenny used the paper cutter to trim Richard's pages.

"Don't cut your fingers," said Richard.

"I promise not to get any blood on your brochure," Jenny said.

While Susan pasted Richard's brochure together, he watched over her shoulder. "You're so good at this," he said.

"I know." Susan smiled up at him.

"I brought the world map that Mrs. Steele said we had to mark up with our route." Richard reached into his backpack and pulled it out.

Susan took the paper and made a face. "The paper is all creased and dirty. You can't hand this in."

Richard shrugged. "I guess it's been in my backpack for a while."

Susan took her notebook out of her bag and pulled out her map. "I can make a copy of my map for you. We have a copier upstairs."

Her mother walked into the kitchen. "Hi, Jenny." She put her hand on Richard's shoulder. "How is your arm?"

"Much better today," Richard said.

"I'll be upstairs," said Susan's mom. "Let me know if you need anything."

After Susan copied the map, she brought her big world atlas to the table.

"I've got the distances for several different routes to India." Richard thumbed through his notebook until he found the page with his mileage calculations.

"How many routes did you find?" Jenny bent over Richard's notebook.

"Three," said Richard. "Rana's plane went through Paris. My way is the long way, around the world through Hawaii, Japan, and China. The shortest route I could find was over the North Pole."

"Planes fly over the North Pole?" Susan was surprised.

"Yes," said Richard, "right over Santa's workshop."

"Rana just wrote that she's really missing the holiday season here," said Susan, "the jolly music, the smell of Christmas trees, the colored lights on houses. And her little sister is worried that Santa won't be able to find them."

"Maybe Rudolph knows the way to Bombay," said Richard. "Hey, it even rhymes."

"Maybe Rana's deer knows the way to Bombay," said Jenny. "He has lights on his antlers."

Susan thought about saying that maybe the deer could *fly* to *Mumbai,* but she decided not to.

"Randy the antlered mule deer, da da da da da da da, Christmas lights in his antlers, da da da da da da da," sang Richard.

"That's a great idea," said Susan. "Let's write a song for Rana and her sister."

"I don't remember all the words to the Rudolph song," said Richard.

"I'll find it on the Internet and print it out," said Susan.

Susan ran upstairs, found the song quickly, and printed out the words. When she got downstairs, Richard and Jenny had already done some more work on the song.

"I thought the deer's name should be Alvin or Arnold," said Jenny.

"Arnold the antlered mule deer," sang Richard. "Felt that he was very strange, Christmas lights in his antlers . . ." Richard stopped. "Now we need something that rhymes with strange."

"Range, like home on the range," suggested Jenny.

Susan started at the beginning of the alphabet, trying to find rhyming words. "Change," she said.

"Hmmm," said Richard.

Susan continued through the alphabet. "Grange, mange." Jenny had already thought of range. "What about deranged?"

"What does that mean?" asked Jenny.

"Crazy, I think," said Susan. "My mother uses it sometimes. She'll say, 'Is that man deranged?'"

"Christmas lights in his antlers," sang Richard, "made him feel like he's deranged? Hmmm. Catchy."

"I don't think most kids will know what it means," said Jenny.

"Okay," said Richard. "Let's start over. How about this? Arnold the antlered mule deer, had something hanging by his eyes, Christmas lights in his antlers . . ."

Richard stopped. "Now we need something that rhymes with eyes."

"Size, rise, cries, lies," said Jenny. "Gave him a case of hives?"

"Made him want to eat french fries?" Richard said, and guffawed.

"What about surprise?" said Susan.

"Well, that was a big surprise," sang Richard. "Yes, that's it."

While Susan wrote those verses down, Richard and Jenny read the song Susan had printed out. Richard thought out loud. "Lots of the other mule deer, snort and jump and trot away, Arnold just dreamed that Santa, would come and make him feel okay."

"I like that," said Jenny.

"On a stormy Christmas Eve, Santa lost his way," suggested Susan.

Richard nodded. "And he said to Arnold, 'I'm trying to find Bombay.'"

"This is great," said Jenny.

Susan wrote the words quickly.

"Arnold turned on his antlers, lighting up the cloudy night," Richard sang off-key. "Soon he was leading Santa, dum de dum de dum de dum."

"Let's see," said Jenny. "Bite rhymes with night. So does kite, light, might, plight."

"What about bright?" said Susan. "Making the way so bright."

Richard nodded. He continued to sing. "Suddenly lots of mule deer, looking up into the sky, dum de dum dum de de dum, for helping Santa Claus to fly."

"Loved their buddy Arnold," Jenny suggested.

"Not enough de dums," said Richard.

"We need something with seven syllables," said Susan. "How about 'praised their good buddy Arnold'?"

"That's it," shouted Richard. "Write that down."

After Susan wrote the rest of the song down, she counted syllables. "Oh, no. 'Making the way so bright' is only six syllables."

Jenny picked up the Rudolph song. She counted with her fingers, moving her lips. "In the last two stanzas, not all the lines are seven syllables either. 'Santa came to say' is only five."

"There you go," said Richard. "No problem. I think our song is great the way it is."

They sang the whole song together.

"I'll send it to Rana tonight," said Susan. "And we can sing it for the class at our holiday party on Friday."

"Tell Rana that we'll put the map by the chimney for Santa," said Richard. "It's only nine thousand two hundred and twenty-nine miles from here to Bombay if you fly over the North Pole."

"How did you figure that out?" asked Susan.

"I just looked at the flight information from the airline that flies that route," said Richard.

Susan was impressed. Richard was really good at writing poems and finding flight information. Of course, she was better at making brochures.

"We can make deer cookies," said Jenny, "and use dots of colored frosting for lights in their antlers."

"I'll help you make them," said Susan.

"I'll help you eat them." Richard wiggled his eyebrows.

"And we can freeze several cookies for Rana and her sister to eat when they come home," Susan said.

"Good idea," said Jenny. "Do you want to bake them Thursday afternoon?"

"No, that's the only day my mom can go Christmas shopping with me," said Susan. "And tomorrow I promised Mary I'd do something with her."

"That's okay," said Jenny. "I'll make the cookies, then we can let the kids in the class decorate their own cookies at the party."

"Maybe we should finish our maps now," Susan suggested. "I think I'll use the route that Rana and her parents took."

Richard consulted his notebook. "It's nine thousand nine hundred and nineteen miles that way."

"Okay. Which route do you want to use, Jenny?"

"I'll use the North Pole route," she said.

"You'll win the prize for the shortest route," said Richard. "And maybe I'll win the longest route. It's eleven thousand five hundred and sixty miles if you go through Honolulu, Beijing, and Hong Kong. I could go through Australia on the way to Bombay and Africa on the way back to make it even longer."

"Which routes do you want me to draw?" said Susan. "I need to finish up here so I can take care of Rana's kitty."

"Well, maybe you can draw the route through Australia for me, and Jenny can draw the one through Africa."

Jenny laughed. "Are we your slaves now?"

Richard looked pained and held up his arm with the green cast. "I need slaves. I'm injured."

Susan felt guilty once again. "Would you like a big slice of coffee cake? My mom just brought it home from the bakery."

She was rewarded with a big grin from Richard.

Chapter 10

After school on Thursday, Susan and her mother went Christmas shopping. At the pet store, they shopped for the animals at Rana's house. Susan picked out blue rocks for Tara's fish and two catnip toys for Tiger. She selected several toys for her own cat, too.

When they'd paid for the purchases, Susan asked, "Do you think we should get something for the birds that come to Rana's feeder?"

"We could put some peanut butter on pinecones and hang them in the trees nearby," suggested her mother.

"Let's hang some of those around our yard, too," said Susan.

"I'll buy an extra jar of peanut butter," said her mother.

On the way home, Susan's mother stopped in front of Rana's house. "Shall I wait for you?"

"No, I've got a lot of things to do today. I want to clean the fish's bowl and put the new rocks inside. I also need to change the kitty's litter box." Susan got out of the car, took the key out of her backpack, and watched her mother drive away.

Tiger was by the door when Susan opened it. She scooped the kitty into her arms and shut the door with her foot. "How are you today, Tiger?"

The cat struggled to get down, then ran toward the kitchen. Susan knew the cat was eager to be fed, so she did that first. Next she wanted to fix Golden Boy's bowl. She put her backpack on the kitchen table, took out the sack from the pet store, and removed the bag of rocks for the fish. She left the catnip toys inside the sack and put it back in her pack. She'd wait until Christmas Day to give the cats their presents.

As Susan climbed the stairs, she worried about Golden Boy. She didn't know much about fish. Had she overfed or underfed him? Had the cat learned to open doors overnight? She was pleased to see that the door to Tara's room was tightly shut. She entered the room and looked around. The fish was still alive, swimming in his big bowl.

Susan filled a small, empty bowl with water from the jug in Tara's closet, then took the net and carefully transferred the fish into it. She carried the large bowl to the bathroom sink and poured out the old water. She peeked out in the hallway to be sure Tiger hadn't come upstairs. No sneaky cat out there. She rinsed the new rocks and placed them on the bottom of the bowl. Then she picked up the bowl and carried it back to the bedroom.

Oh, no, the kitty was on Tara's dresser. She had her nose inside the little fishbowl. With her pink tongue, she was slurping the water. "Tiger,

no," shouted Susan as she set the larger bowl down.

The cat stopped drinking and looked at Susan.

Susan grabbed Tiger and took her out of the room. She let out a big sigh. "You are such a naughty kitty." She carried the cat downstairs and put her on the kitchen floor. The cat walked over to her plate. It was empty. "Murrrr," said the cat. She looked up at Susan.

"You must be really hungry today," said Susan, spooning more tuna feast onto the plate.

She hurried back upstairs to get the fish safely into its big bowl. "How do you like your new rocks?" she said after she'd netted Golden Boy and returned him to his redecorated bowl. She shut the door and pulled on it to be sure it was tightly closed. Golden Boy didn't know how close he'd come to being a cat snack.

Downstairs again, Susan looked out the window at the bird feeder. Underneath it, she saw the mule deer. He was eating the birdseed that had spilled out of the overturned trash can. In all the excitement after Richard's accident, Susan had forgotten to set the can upright and put the lid back on. The deer kept eating and eating. And she had just learned that it was illegal to feed deer. She could be fined. Or maybe even put in jail. She hadn't thought to ask the wildlife man about the punishment for feeding deer. She considered chasing the deer away but decided that was too dangerous. Later, after the deer was finished eating, she'd go outside and take care of the can.

This cat-sitting job was much harder than she'd imagined. Of course, it was more than taking care of a cat. She also had to take care of a fish and wild birds and a mule deer with Christmas lights in his antlers.

She entered the family room and looked at the jeans and sweatshirt nest she had made for the kitty. Oh, yuck! The cat had barfed all over the clothes. And that wasn't all. The sweatshirt was covered with a thick mat of gray hairs.

Susan sighed again and carried the sweatshirt and jeans to the kitchen sink. She scraped the cat barf into the sink with a knife, then tried picking off the cat hairs. This was going to take forever.

She called her mother. "Mom, remember that sweatshirt of Rana's I put on the floor for the cat? Well, it's covered in kitty barf and millions of cat hairs. I've scraped off the throw up, but I need something to get the hair off."

"I don't want to add a hairy stained sweatshirt

to my wash." Her mother hesitated. "Why don't I bring you a lint roller and a good stain remover? Then I'll help you start the washer at Rana's house."

As soon as her mother arrived, Susan started trying to remove the cat hairs. It took forever to get all the hair off the sweatshirt. Fortunately, the kitty throw up came off easily with the stain remover. Susan's mother started the washer, then turned to her daughter. "I need to go home and grade the exams," she said, "but I'll set the dryer dials so that all you have to do is put the clothes inside and push this button." She pointed to a black button.

After her mother left, Susan watered the plants, dumped out the used kitty litter, and poured new litter into the kitty's litter box. Then she pulled a book from her pack and read it. The cat sat on the couch beside her.

After reading several chapters, she went to check on the clothes. She lifted the pants from the washer and leaned down to pull the door of the dryer open. She tossed the pants inside.

Her cell phone rang, and she went to answer it. Her mother had decided to order pizza for dinner and wondered what she'd like on it. "Mushrooms and green peppers," she told her mother.

Susan went back to the washer and shook out the sweatshirt, so she could see if the stains were really gone. The sweatshirt looked good. Without bending over, she tossed it into the dryer, shut the door, and pushed the button. *Ker-thump! Ker-thump!* went the dryer. Her mother's dryer never sounded like that. Something must be wrong. She opened the dryer door. Before she could lean over to look inside, Tiger leaped out of the dryer like she'd been shot out of a cannon. Susan could barely breathe. Her heart thumped in her chest. She'd almost killed the cat!

Chapter 11

Susan ran into the kitchen trying to find the cat. "Tiger!" she called. "Tiger! Where are you?" She raced through the house, looking in every place she'd ever seen the kitty. She couldn't find her anywhere.

She called her mother. "Mom, the cat sneaked into the dryer when I wasn't looking. I turned it on and heard an awful thumping noise. When I opened the dryer, the cat leaped out and ran away. I can't find her anywhere. I'm the worst cat-sitter in the whole world." And then she started to cry.

"I'll be right there," said her mother.

Susan was so relieved when her mother arrived. Together they searched the house. They couldn't find Tiger.

"Let's check under the beds again," said Susan.

"Remember how Portia hides under my bed sometimes after seeing the vet and having her teeth cleaned?"

"I have a flashlight in the car," said her mother. "Let's try using that."

After her mother retrieved the flashlight, they went upstairs to Rana's bedroom. Susan lay down on the floor by Rana's bed and lifted the flowered bed skirt. She shone the light under the bed. Two bright eyes gleamed back.

"Come out, little kitty," said Susan. "I'm so sorry I hurt you."

But the kitty wouldn't budge from her hiding spot.

Susan's mother brought some cat food upstairs. Still the cat wouldn't come out.

"Maybe if I set the fishbowl on the floor, she'll come out," said Susan.

She went into Tara's room and carefully carried the fishbowl next door. Sure enough, the cat crawled out. Susan picked her up and held her close. "Are you okay, kitty?" she said softly.

Her mother took the cat and looked her over.

Susan put the fishbowl safely back on the shelf in Tara's room.

"I think we should stay here for several hours and just watch her." Susan's mother carried the cat to the family room. "I'll run home and bring some pizza for us to eat."

"Okay." Susan sat on the couch and reached for the cat. "I'll hold her until you get back. If she'll let me." The kitty sat down on Susan's lap. She didn't purr, but she didn't try to run away.

About fifteen minutes later, Susan's mother returned. She carried a large pizza box. "I left some for your father and brought the rest." She put the box in the middle of the kitchen table.

Susan moved the cat from her lap to a couch cushion. Then she took two plates from the cabinet by the sink and set them on the table. She and her mother sat down to eat. Susan's mother put a piece of pizza on each plate, then closed the lid.

Suddenly, Tiger leaped onto the table. "Well, she can still jump," said Susan's mother. "That's a good sign."

Tiger sniffed the pizza box. She stood on top of the box, then sat down on it, continuing to sniff. Her muzzle moved back and forth.

Susan and her mother laughed.

"Maybe we should let her sit there for a while,"

said Susan's mother. "The warm box probably feels good if her body is bruised."

Susan was surprised. Her mother never let their cat on tables. But when Tiger tried to steal some pizza from her plate, Susan told the cat, "No," and put her down on the floor.

After dinner, Susan read her book again while her mother read some magazines. The cat sat on the couch for a while, then jumped down and went into the kitchen. Susan followed her. The cat ate some cat food and took a drink of water from her bowl.

"Tiger's eating and drinking," Susan said. "I think she's feeling better."

"We'll wait for the dryer to finish," said her mother, "and if the cat's still okay, we can both go home."

When the dryer shut off, Susan went to check on the clothes. As she walked back through the kitchen, she saw the cat. Tiger was rolling around on the floor, playing with something. Susan leaned over her. The cat held a torn plastic bag of catnip between her paws. Susan's backpack lay on the floor where she had left it, but the sack that had contained the presents was torn open and lay near the pack.

"That crazy cat must have smelled the catnip in my pack," said Susan.

Her mother stood beside her. "What a little monster!"

Susan nodded. "Yes, she is. But I think that means she's feeling better. Now we can go home."

Chapter 12

Susan's mother drove her to school on Friday. On the way, they stopped to check on Tiger. The cat met Susan at the door as usual, ran down the hall into the kitchen, then stood waiting by her dish. Tiger was so excited about eating that the end of her tail quivered. Susan knelt down and patted her. She was relieved that the cat could still run and was behaving normally.

Susan opened the pantry and took two cans of cat food from the shelf. She knelt again and offered both cans to Tiger. "Which one would you like today?" she asked. "Tasty tender chicken or hearty beef and liver?"

The cat smelled both cans. She nosed one of the cans again and rubbed her face on it. Susan opened that can and gave the cat a big helping of chicken.

When Susan got out of the car at school, a cold

blast of wind blew her hair across her face. She brushed her hair from her eyes and found Jenny and Richard huddled beside a large spruce tree close to the entrance.

"How are all of Rana's animals today?" Richard asked. "The deer hasn't lost his antlers yet, has he?"

"No, the deer still has his antlers and the Christmas lights are still attached. The fish is fine, too." Susan tried to smile, but couldn't. "I hope the cat is all right."

"Did something happen to the kitty?" asked Jenny.

Susan hadn't planned ever to say anything to anyone about the cat in the dryer, but she found herself telling Jenny and Richard. "I was putting some of Rana's clothes in the dryer, because the cat threw up on them, and I had to wash them. Somehow the cat sneaked into the dryer when I wasn't looking."

"Oh, kind of like a kitty Ferris wheel ride?" Richard chuckled.

Jenny poked him in the ribs. "Richard, the poor cat must have been terrified."

"She shot out of the dryer when I opened the door," said Susan. "I felt terrible. I was responsible for her and I didn't do a good job."

"But she's okay, right?" said Richard.

"Yes, she seemed fine this morning."

"So no harm done," Richard continued. "Hey, you know that saying 'Curiosity killed the cat'? I bet she's not the first cat to get into a dryer."

"Do you think so?" Susan said.

"I really do." Richard patted her shoulder.

Kids started filing into the school, so Susan hurried inside with her friends. She stomped her feet and shivered as they walked down the warm hallway to the classroom.

Since it was the last day of school before Christmas vacation, Mrs. Steele had brought a small fir tree to school with tiny red balls and bows all over it. She had removed the pencil jar and all the usual books and papers from her desk and covered it with a red tablecloth. She was even wearing a red sweater with Santa, his sleigh, and reindeer flying across it.

Their teacher loved the song about Arnold the mule deer when Susan showed it to her. She asked Susan and Jenny to write the words on several big sheets of paper. "Then the whole class can sing it during the party this afternoon," she said.

While Susan and Jenny worked on preparations for the holiday party, the rest of the class worked on their brochures. Susan felt good about finishing her brochure early and also helping her two friends to finish as well. Their brochures looked better than anyone else's in the whole class. She was glad she could be proud of something. She certainly didn't feel good about cat-sitting.

Richard helped Kevin and other students find information on the Internet for their maps. Nobody else had a trip to as many countries as Richard, so he won the prizes for the highest mileage and the most countries visited. Jenny won the prize for the shortest trip. Susan was proud of her friends. Of course, she could have won if she'd wanted to.

After lunch, several parents came to the classroom to help with the party. Susan's mother brought paper cups and fruit juice. Jenny had the deer cookies on a big metal pan that had been covered with red foil. She had also brought tubes of green, red, and yellow frosting to decorate the deer's antlers.

"I'm ready for my cookie," said Richard.

"Not yet," said Jenny. "We have to sing first."

Richard pretended to cry.

Mrs. Steele stood in front of the room. "I want everyone to come up front and sit on the rug. Susan and Richard and Jenny are going to tell you all about a song they wrote."

Susan spoke first. "I got an e-mail from Rana several days ago. She said it didn't feel like Christmas at all in India. And her sister, Tara, is worried that Santa won't find them there and that her stocking will be empty on Christmas morning."

"That's silly," said Kevin. "Her parents can just stick something in her stocking."

"It wouldn't be the same as having Santa come." Susan glared at Kevin before continuing. "Anyway, there was a mule deer in Rana's yard every day when I stopped by to take care of the cat. The poor deer had Christmas lights in his antlers. I wanted to help him, but the man from the wildlife department told me never to go near a wild deer."

"What about Santa's reindeer?" said Kevin. "Can you go near them?"

"I'd suggest staying off rooftops, especially at night when Santa lands his sleigh up there." Richard grinned.

"So since we couldn't help the deer," Susan said, "we came up with the idea to write a song about him. We named the deer Arnold."

"That's a dumb name for a deer," muttered Kevin.

"Kevin, you're supposed to be listening," said Mrs. Steele. "Susan and Jenny and Richard will

98

sing their song for you first, then we'll all sing it."
She pointed to the board, where she had fastened
the sheets of paper with the words:

Arnold the antlered mule deer
Had something hanging by his eyes,
Christmas lights in his antlers,
Well, that was a big surprise.

Lots of the other mule deer,
Snort and jump and trot away.
Arnold just dreamed that Santa
Would come and make him feel okay.

On a stormy Christmas Eve,
Santa lost his way.
And he said to Arnold,
"I'm trying to find Bombay."

Arnold turned on his antlers,
Lighting up the cloudy night.
Soon he was leading Santa,
Making the way so bright.

Suddenly lots of mule deer,
Looking up into the sky,

Praised their good buddy Arnold,
For helping Santa Claus to fly.

Susan's voice shook when she sang the first verse, but then she saw Mary smiling. Her voice was stronger when she sang the next verse. By the end, she was belting the song out just like Richard.

The class clapped when the singers finished.

"I like your song," said Mary. "I'm sure Rana and Tara will like it, too."

Susan hoped that was true. She hadn't had an e-mail from Rana for several days.

"Now let's all sing the song together," said Mrs. Steele.

Richard directed the singing by waving his green-casted arm like a conductor's baton.

"Now it's time to eat the cookies." Richard headed for the refreshments.

"Wait," said Susan. "Jenny and I will show everyone how to put frosting on the cookies."

Susan rushed over to the table and grabbed a tube of frosting. "You put tiny dots of frosting on the antlers, so it looks like Christmas lights."

Richard was clumsy with the frosting. His dots looked more like huge spotlights. "Tastes good anyway," he said, taking a big bite.

Mary put dainty dots of green and red frosting on her cookie. "This is such fun," she said.

"I love your snowman earrings," said Susan. She had helped Mary pick them out at the store.

"I love your silver snowflake earrings," said Mary.

Kevin grabbed a tube of red frosting and made squiggly red lines all over his cookie.

Susan glared at him, but didn't say anything. Then she fixed another cookie for Richard, making perfect little dots all along the deer's antlers.

After school, Susan went to Rana's house again to check on the cat. Tiger ran to meet her and, after an afternoon snack, sat on her lap. Susan combed the cat's silky fur. Tiger lay on her side and purred

and purred. Susan rolled the cat over so that she could comb the other side of the cat's back. The cat closed her eyes and purred some more. The end of her pink, dimpled tongue hung out of her mouth. The cat must have forgotten all about her horrible experience in the dryer. Or else she didn't know that it was Susan's fault.

When Susan got home, she discovered a new e-mail from Rana. "We've been singing your deer song every night with Tara. She's been drawing pictures of the deer leading Santa's reindeer. Thank you so much for taking care of Tiger, Golden Boy, and Arnold the deer. My dad calls you our fabulous critter-sitter."

Susan didn't feel very fabulous. She printed out the e-mail to show her mother.

Her mother was grading papers, but she looked up when Susan entered the dining room.

"Rana's dad thinks I'm a good pet-sitter," Susan said. She couldn't bring herself to say fabulous.

Her mother patted her hand. "You are. The kitty and the fish are still alive and well. The birds outside are eating birdseed and are probably enjoying the peanut butter pinecones we hung in the trees. And the mule deer buck is okay, too."

"I try so hard to do everything right," said Susan.

"Sometimes you learn by making mistakes," said her mother. "Nobody's perfect. Life is full of things you don't expect, like cats jumping into dryers or boys falling out of trees. When things went wrong, you did the right thing. And, as Shakespeare wrote, 'All's well that ends well.'" Her mother gave her a warm smile.

Susan smiled back. She had certainly made

some mistakes, but she had learned from them. She wasn't a perfect cat-sitter, but she probably wasn't a terrible one either. Maybe she was actually a pretty good cat-sitter. And that was good enough.